FEB 0 9 2023

Gray Fox in the Moonlight

WRITTEN & ILLUSTRATED BY

ISAAC PETERSON

THE
collective
BOOK STUDIO

Gray Fox
walks

so lightly

through the woods.

The breeze

moves slightly.

Autumn leaves fall.

Gray Fox looks up at the sky.

The stars shine

between

the

leaves.

The moon
is caught

in the
branches.

Gray Fox
sees

the river unwind
between the trees.

The water reflects
Gray Fox's eyes.

All the world is still

until

Gray Fox moves again.

The path

bends

back.

Gray Fox runs swiftly.

She leaps the log.

Back
again

to her den.

Where
her kits

Fall asleep
Gray Fox.

The sun
is rising.

ABOUT THE AUTHOR

Isaac Peterson grew up in Alaska and loves comics, painting, and photography. Ruby Peterson, his daughter, drew or painted many of the background elements in this book. Isaac and Ruby love working on projects together.

ISBN: 978-1-68555-032-5
Ebook ISBN: 978-1-68555-033-2
LCCN: 2022936368

MIX
Paper from responsible sources
FSC® C102842

Printed using Forest Stewardship Council certified stock from sustainably managed forests.

Manufactured in China.

Design by AJ Hansen.

1 3 5 7 9 10 8 6 4 2

The Collective Book Studio®
Oakland, California
www.thecollectivebook.studio

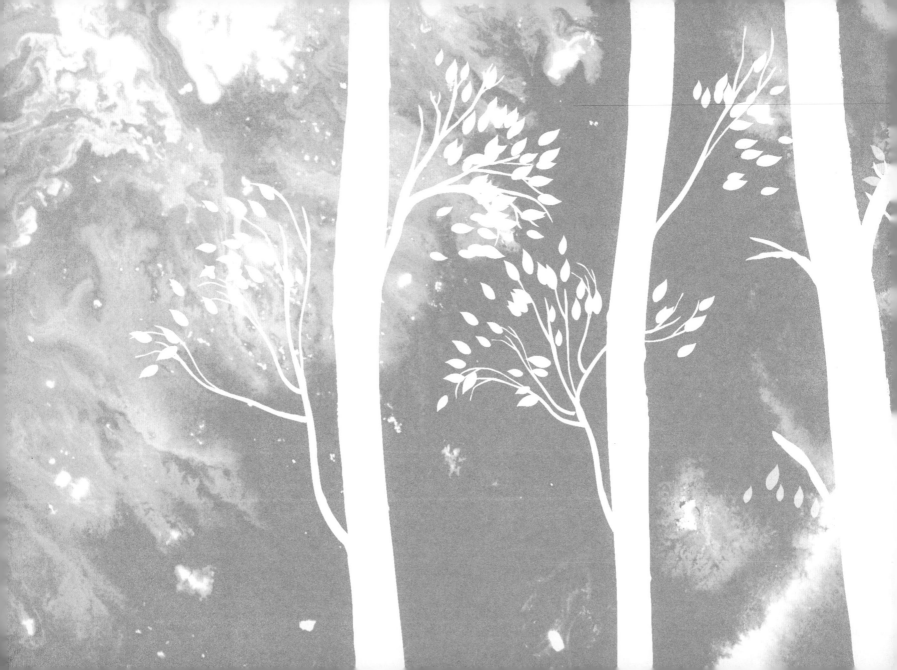